This edition published by Parragon Books
Unit 13–17, Avonbridge Trading Estate, Atlantic Road, Avonmouth, Bristol, BS11 9QD

© 1994 Twin Books Limited

Produced by Twin Books Limited
Kimbolton House, 117a Fulham Road, London, SW3 6RL, England

Directed by CND- Muriel Nathan-Deiller
Illustrated by Van Gool-Lefèvre-Loiseaux

ISBN 0 75250 085 6

Printed and bound in Italy

Sleeping Beauty

Many years ago there lived a king and queen. Together they ruled wisely over their kingdom. The king and queen loved each other very much, but there was one thing that spoiled their happiness – they had no children. Both of them wanted very much to have a child, but for many years their only companion was a small dog, called Jester. Every evening, after the dog and all their servants were asleep, the king and queen would sigh deeply, and wish for a child to brighten their castle.

One day the king and queen's dearest wish finally came true, and the queen gave birth to a beautiful baby girl. The king could hardly contain his joy, and danced merrily about the castle, calling on everyone to come and see the new princess. Then he rushed back to his daughter's side. "You are so beautiful and precious!" he exclaimed to the sleeping baby. Then he called for his servants. "We must hold a royal party in honour of my daughter," he told them. "All the fairies in the kingdom shall be invited to share in our happiness!"

The day was set for the party, and royal messengers hurried to all corners of the kingdom to deliver the invitations.

Everyone in the castle was busy. The cooks squabbled in the kitchens as they prepared their most delicious dishes. The maids sang and laughed as they got the great ballroom and banqueting hall ready for the feast. Finally the day arrived and the fairies flew into the castle, by various magical means, to celebrate the birth of the royal baby.

As soon as they arrived, each of the fairies hurried to peek into the royal cradle, smiling in delight at the tiny princess. Then they took their seats at the long banqueting table, and the feast began. The king sat in his jewelled throne at the head of the table, and after filling his goblet with the finest wine in the land, he proposed a toast to his daughter. "To a long and happy life for our little princess!" he proclaimed. The guests cheered and clapped so loudly that it is a wonder they didn't wake the sleeping baby!

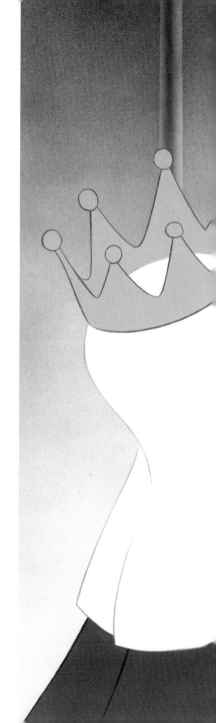

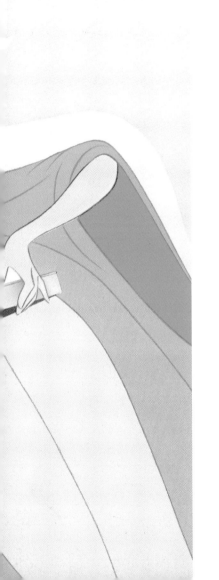

The party was a huge success. Everyone enjoyed the delicious feast, and soon all the fairies were dancing merrily to the music of a lively band. When the little princess awoke, the king took her in his arms and danced with her all around the room, much to the fairies' delight.

Then the king ordered the music to stop, and gathered the fairies together. He gave each of them a box of glittering jewels to thank them for coming. All the fairies agreed that there had never been such a kind and generous king.

But suddenly the joyful celebration was rudely interrupted. The ballroom doors flew open and a dark, sinister figure stormed across the floor. It was the evil and most powerful fairy in the kingdom. The king and queen were horrified. In their joy and excitement they had quite forgotten to invite her to the party. She glared angrily at the innocent baby, then turned to face the other fairies.

"Go ahead and give the child your gifts," she hissed, with an evil smile. "And then I have a present of my own for the little princess."

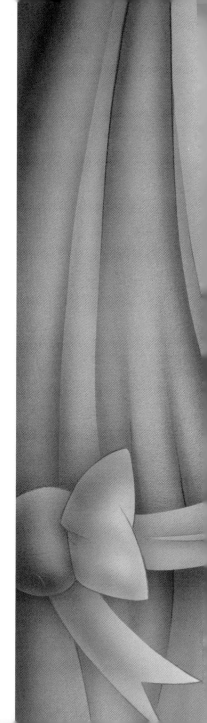

The evil fairy sat glowering in a corner of the room. The king and queen and the other fairies tried to ignore her and carry on with the party, but the happy mood was spoiled. One by one the fairies approached the baby princess, bestowing magical gifts such as beauty, kindness and wisdom. The smallest fairy did not present her gift with the others. She knew that the evil fairy was up to no good, so she hid behind the cradle and waited to see what she was planning.

Then the evil fairy stalked across the room. Drawing herself up to an enormous height, she began to weave her wicked spell. The king and queen gasped in horror as she conjured up an image of the little princess as she would look as a young woman.

"Hear this!" she snarled. "This is my gift. When the princess has become a young lady, she will prick her thumb on a spindle, and she will die!" Then before anyone had a chance to stop her, the evil fairy swept out of the castle.

The king and queen begged the fairies to help them, but they shook their heads. "We have already given our gifts," they said sadly. "We cannot use our magic again." Then the smallest fairy stepped out from behind the cradle.

"The evil fairy is so powerful that I cannot undo her spell," she whispered to the shocked crowd. "But I can soften it a little." And she waved her magic wand around the sleeping baby, saying, "Princess, when the spindle pricks your thumb you will not die, but will sleep for a hundred years. Only a prince's kiss may awaken you."

The king and queen were determined to do all they could to protect their child from harm. The king sent his heralds throughout the royal kingdom, where they proclaimed that all spinning wheels must be brought to the cobbled castle courtyard and burned. Soon a huge fire was raging, as the king's loyal subjects obeyed his command.

"Now nothing can hurt our little girl," sighed the king with relief, but the queen was not sure that the evil fairy would be thwarted so easily.

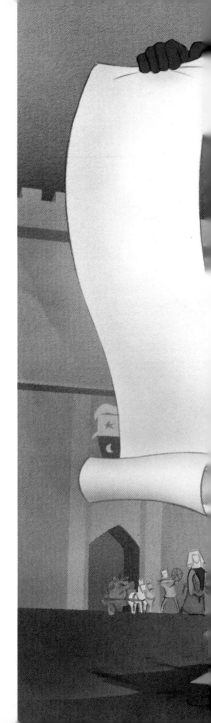

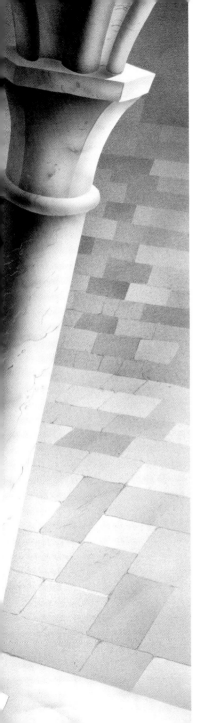

The years passed, and the baby grew into a lovely young woman. Her heart was kind and good, and she was loved by all. The king and queen had never told their daughter of the evil fairy's spell. At first they had not wanted to frighten her, but now their life was so happy that they had almost forgotten about it.

One day they set out on a tour of their kingdom, leaving the princess in the care of Jester and the castle servants. The princess waved them goodbye as their carriage drove through the castle gates.

While she was playing with Jester in the courtyard, the princess discovered a stairway that she had never seen before. It led up into an old tower, where no one ever went. She loved to explore the castle, and climbed eagerly up the winding stairs. The sunlight dissolved into a gloomy darkness at the top of the staircase, and the princess could just make out a wooden door, which was shut tight. The curious princess could hear something on the other side of the door, and as she reached out for the handle, it swung slowly open.

In the cold, dark room on the other side of the door, an old woman, hidden in a cloak, sat spinning by candlelight. The princess was a little nervous, for she did not recognise the woman, and had never seen a spinning wheel before. At her side, Jester whimpered.

"Come closer, my dear," invited the old woman. "Would you like to try it?"

The princess stepped inside, and slowly crossed the room, Jester at her heels. The old woman began to smile.

"You must take this spindle, my dear," crooned the old woman.

But as the princess reached out, the sharp point of the spindle pricked her thumb. At once a wave of tiredness overcame the princess, and she fell to the ground in a deep sleep. With a triumphant cackle, the old woman pushed back her hood, revealing the frightening face of the evil fairy.

"Now I have had my revenge!" she said, and still laughing, she fled down the stairway and out of the castle.

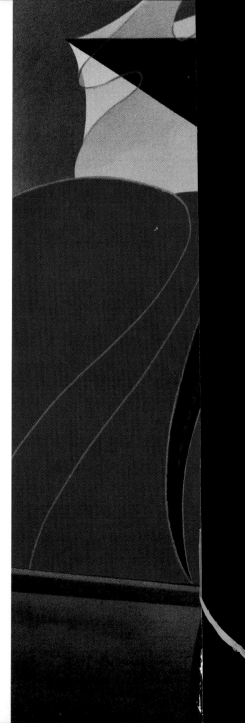

Later that day, the king and queen returned from their trip, and were surprised that their beloved daughter did not run out to greet them. When they discovered that none of the servants had seen her all day, they began to worry.

"Where is Jester?" asked the king. "He never leaves her side." Suddenly they heard barking, and Jester came running across the courtyard. They followed the little dog up the stairway, where they found their daughter on the floor by the spinning wheel. Sadly they carried the princess to her room, and lay her on her bed.

35

The whole castle was plunged into sadness, and the king and queen were in despair. Then the queen remembered the smallest fairy, and her words at the party, and called for the royal messenger. She ordered him to go to the fairy and beg her to help them once more.

The messenger bounded across the kingdom in his seven league boots until he found the fairy. Wiping a tear from his eye, he said, "Please, you must come quickly! The princess has fallen under an evil spell."

With her pet birds pulling the hem of her long dress, and the messenger balanced in her skirt, she flew to the castle. There she found the beautiful princess, deep in a dreamless sleep, and watched over by her unhappy parents.

"Thank you for coming," said the king sadly, "I thought she would be safe here, but the evil fairy has won."

The smallest fairy shook her head. "I have an idea," she said. "If everyone in the castle were to sleep for a hundred years, then nothing will have changed when the princess awakens."

"Please, do anything you can to help our dear daughter," begged the king. So the little fairy flitted throughout the castle, casting a magic spell that put everyone into a deep slumber.

First she visited the kitchens, and waving her magic wand, she set to work. The cooks with their pots and pans, the butlers with their dishes, the maids with their sewing and cleaning – all of them fell fast asleep where they stood, frozen in time.

The guards at the great castle gates, the queen's ladies in waiting and the courtiers – everyone was soon fast asleep. It was quite a big spell for such a small fairy, and she was very tired, but satisfied with her work.

"Now no one will age during the princess's long sleep," she said to herself. "Everything will remain unchanged until the prince comes to awaken her." Then she wearily left the silent castle, and returned to her home.

Night came, then day, and nothing stirred in the castle. A week passed, then a month, then years came and went. Still all slumbered on under the enchantment of the little fairy's spell. The trees grew tall, and vines and brambles wound around the branches until the castle was hidden behind a thick, impenetrable barrier.

A hundred years passed, and the castle stood almost forgotten by the inhabitants of the surrounding countryside.

One day a handsome prince from a nearby kingdom was riding through the forest. He spied the towers of a castle in the distance, and when he came across a peasant working in his field he asked how he could reach it.

The old man laughed. "No one can enter that castle," he said. "It is all grown over with brambles. They say the whole place is under an enchantment, and everyone's been sleeping for a hundred years." And he told the Prince about the wicked fairy's spell.

47

The prince didn't believe him. "I heard that story years ago!" he exclaimed. "It's nothing but a fairy tale."

But the old man's words had made him even more curious about the castle, and he was determined to see for himself. As he approached, the thorny brambles flattened themselves to the ground by some strange magic. A pathway appeared, leading straight to the castle gates. Intrigued, the prince followed the path, and stepped up to the entrance.

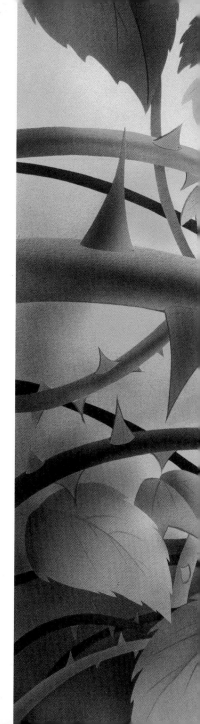

Cautiously the prince pushed open the heavy castle doors. As soon as he stepped inside, he realized that the old story was true. In every room people were frozen in a deep sleep. Their clothes were old-fashioned and everything was covered in dust and cobwebs. The prince gazed around him in amazement.

"They really have been sleeping for a hundred years!" he whispered to himself, hardly daring to disturb the unearthly quiet. "I wonder how I can wake them?"

He wandered through the silent castle until he came into the room of the slumbering princess. He walked slowly to her bed, and stood looking down at her sadly. She looked as if she might awaken at any moment. Then he knelt at her side. "You truly are a sleeping beauty," he whispered, overcome by her loveliness.

Gently he leaned over, and kissed her on the cheek. Then, saddened by what he'd seen, the prince stood up and turned to leave the room.

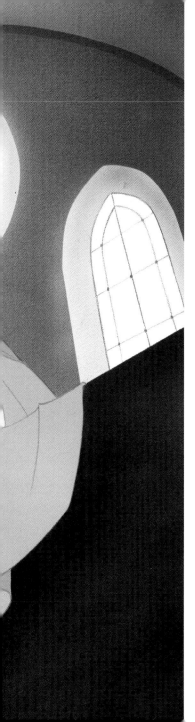

Suddenly there was a gentle sigh behind him. The prince whirled round, and to his astonishment saw that the princess had opened her eyes.

"Who are you?" she asked. The prince told her who he was, and how he came to be there. The princess's eyes grew round with wonder as he told her about the wicked fairy's spell, and how she had slept for one hundred years. "And you woke me," she whispered, feeling love growing in her heart for this handsome prince.

As soon as the prince had broken the spell with his kiss, everyone in the castle had also come to life. The king and queen rushed to their daughter's bedroom, where they were overjoyed to find the princess awake. When they saw the prince who had ended the enchantment they were delighted, and begged him to join them for a feast. The servants bustled around, cleaning and tidying the castle, and preparing food. The prince accepted their invitation, then shyly asked if he might marry their daughter.

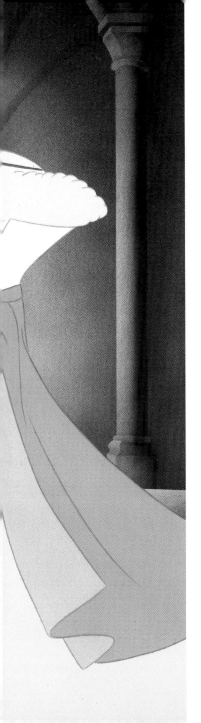

The king and queen agreed joyfully, and decreed that on the seventh day the prince and princess would be married. Invitations were sent out to friends and family, and to the fairies of the kingdom. The smallest fairy of all was to be their special guest of honour.

They had no fear of the wicked fairy spoiling their party this time, for when she had heard that the spell was broken, she had left the kingdom in a rage!

And so the prince and his sleeping beauty
were married. All the kingdom rejoiced with the
happy couple, and for many days the castle was
filled with laughter and music. Such merry
sounds had not been heard for a hundred years,
and everyone agreed that a happier celebration
had never been seen.